Frédéric
Brrémaud

Federico
Bertolucci

# Little
# TAILS

## In the Jungle

### with
### Chipper & Squizzo

**WRITTEN BY**
**FRÉDÉRIC BRRÉMAUD**

**ILLUSTRATED BY**
**FEDERICO BERTOLUCCI**

**TRANSLATION ADAPTED BY**
**MIKE KENNEDY**

**MAGNETIC PRESS**

MIKE KENNEDY, *President/Publisher*

WES HARRIS, *Vice President*

DAVID DISSANAYAKE, *PR & Marketing*

4910 N. WINTHROP AVE #3S

CHICAGO, IL  60640

WWW.MAGNETIC-PRESS.COM

**LITTLE TAILS** IN THE JUNGLE (VOLUME 2)
SEPTEMBER 2016. FIRST PRINTING
ISBN: 978-1-942367-26-0

FIRST PUBLISHED IN FRANCE BY EDITIONS CLAIR DE LUNE
ALL CONTENT © 2014 FRÉDÉRIC BRRÉMAUD AND FEDERICO BERTOLUCCI

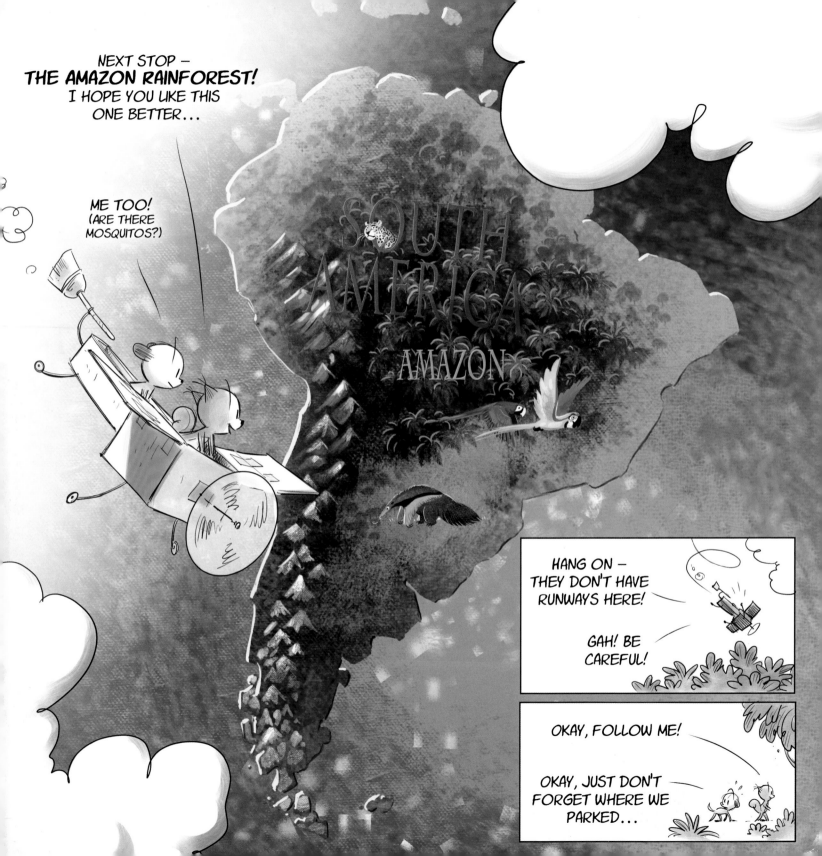

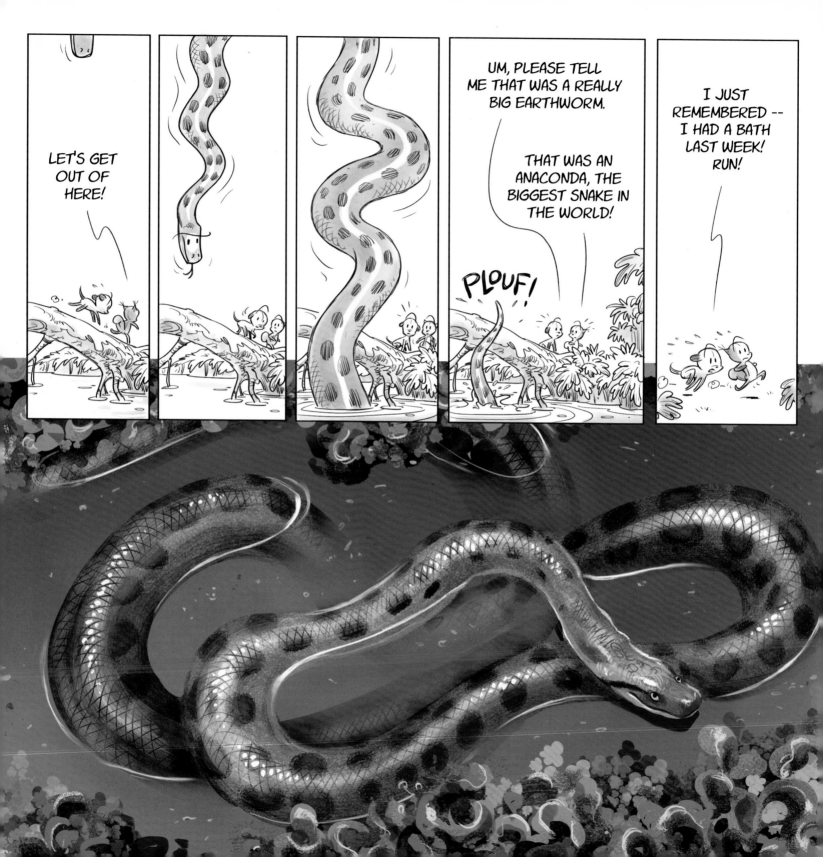

## TOUCAN

THE TOUCAN IS A BEAUTIFUL BIRD, BUT ISN'T THAT LARGE BEAK TOO HEAVY FOR HIS HEAD? NOPE! IT IS HOLLOW AND MADE OF KERATIN (LIKE OUR FINGERNAILS)! THE SIZE OF THE BEAK HELPS IT REACH FRUIT AT THE END OF FARAWAY FLIMSY BRANCHES. IT ALSO HELPS THEM KEEP AN EVEN BODY TEMPERATURE BY STORING WARM AIR IN THE WINTER OR RELEASING BODY HEAT IN THE SUMMER!

## HOWLER MONKEY

THE HOWLER MONKEY IS CONSIDERED THE LOUDEST ANIMAL IN THE JUNGLE. YOU CAN HEAR HIS LOUD CRY FOR MILES! IT IS HOW THEY CAN COMMUNICATE WITH EACH OTHER OVER LONG DISTANCES, AND HOW THEY PROTECT THEIR FRIENDS AND TERRITORY. WHEN ONE SPOTS TROUBLE, HE'LL BEGAN TO HOOT AND HOWL, WARNING EVERYONE OF THE DANGER! THEN HE'LL RUN AWAY, THROWING STUFF AT THE ATTACKERS! SOMETIMES IT'S BEST TO CRY FOR HELP AND RUN AWAY!

## JAGUAR

THE JAGUAR IS A BIG CAT WHO CAN GROW AS LARGE AS A HUMAN AND WEIGH UP TO 200 POUNDS! THEY LIKE TO HUNT ON RIVER BANKS, WHERE THEY ARE KNOWN TO PREY ON ALL KINDS OF ANIMALS. ITS JAWS ARE POWERFUL ENOUGH TO CRACK A TURTLE SHELL! THE NAME "JAGUAR" COMES FROM THE TUPI-GUARANI AMAZON INDIAN WORD "YAGUARETE", WHICH MEANS "THE BEAST THAT KILLS ITS PREY WITH ONE BOUND."

IT SAYS HERE THAT THE WORD "YAGUARA" ALSO SOMETIMES MEANS "DOG"...!

THEY PROBABLY DON'T MEAN "LITTLE PUPPY THAT SLEEPS IN A BASKET"...

## BLACK PANTHER

CONTRARY TO POPULAR BELIEF, THE BLACK PANTHER ISN'T A DIFFERENT KIND OF CAT, IT IS ACTUALLY A TYPE OF LEOPARD OR JAGUAR THAT HAPPENS TO HAVE BLACK FUR. THEY ALSO HAVE STRIPES OR SPOTS, LIKE THEIR COUSINS, BUT BECAUSE OF A GENETIC PIGMENTATION THAT MAKES THEIR FUR DARK, WE CAN'T SEE THEM. AND SINCE IT IS A GENETIC DIFFERENCE, LIKE HAIR COLOR, A BLACK PANTHER MOM CAN GIVE BIRTH TO A REGULAR SPOTTED LEOPARD CUB.

## SLOTH

THE SLOTH HAS TWO MORE VERTEBRAE THAN OTHER MAMMALS, AND HAS ONE OF THE MOST FLEXIBLE NECKS IN THE WORLD. LIKE THE OWL, HE CAN ALMOST TURN HIS HEAD TO SEE HIS OWN BACK! THEY MOVE VERY SLOWLY AND SPEND THEIR LIVES CLINGING TO TREES, ONLY CLIMBING TO THE GROUND WHEN IT HAS TO. FORTUNATELY, THEY DIGEST FOOD VERY SLOWLY, SO THEY DON'T HAVE TO MOVE AROUND A LOT! IN FACT, THEY CAN SLEEP UP TO 19 HOURS A DAY!

WOW, CAN YOU IMAGINE SLEEPING 19 HOURS A DAY? CHIPPER...?

## ASIAN ELEPHANT

THE ASIAN ELEPHANT IS SMALLER THAN ITS AFRICAN COUSIN, WHICH IS THE LARGEST LAND ANIMAL ON THE PLANET. STILL PLENTY BIG, THIS SMALLER COUSIN IS ALSO RECOGNIZED IN HIS SMALLER EARS. HE LIKES TO WALK IN THE FOREST IN SEARCH OF THE BEST PLANTS TO EAT, AND HE USUALLY LIVES IN A GROUP, OFTEN GUIDED BY AN OLDER FEMALE. IT MAKES SENSE — THE OLDER ELEPHANT KNOWS WHERE ALL THE BEST TRAILS ARE!

THE TIGER IS THE LARGEST OF ALL THE BIG CATS. IT CAN MEASURE UP TO 10 FEET IN LENGTH AND WEIGH UP TO 850 POUNDS! THEIR STRIPES ARE NOT ONLY BEAUTIFUL, BUT VERY USEFUL FOR CAMOUFLAGE IN THE JUNGLE. THERE ARE SEVERAL DIFFERENT KINDS OF TIGERS FOUND THROUGHOUT ASIA: THE **BENGAL TIGER**, WHICH IS THE MOST COMMON TYPE FOUND IN INDIA AND BANGLADESH; THE **CORBETT TIGER**, FOUND IN SOUTHEAST ASIA; THE **SUMATRAN TIGER**, ONLY FOUND ON THE ISLAND OF SUMATRA; THE **XIAMEN TIGER**, WHICH IS A SMALLER COUSIN FOUND IN CHINA; AND THE BIGGEST OF ALL TIGERS, THE **SIBERIAN TIGER** FOUND (OF COURSE) IN SIBERIA. THERE WERE ONCE OTHERS, TOO, BUT THEY HAVE ALL UNFORTUNATELY DISAPPEARED.

AS CITIES GROW, HUMANS MOVE INTO THEIR TERRITORY, DESTROYING THE JUNGLE AND LEAVING LESS SPACE FOR TIGERS TO LIVE. SOME HUMANS ALSO HUNT TIGERS FOR THEIR FUR AND OUT OF FEAR. BECAUSE OF THIS, THE TIGER HAS BECOME NEARLY EXTINCT. TODAY, THERE ARE LESS THAN 4000 TIGERS IN THE WILD. THANKS TO ORGANIZATIONS LIKE **PLANET TIGRE**, **WORLD WILDLIFE FUND**, AND **THE PANTHERA CORPORATION**, PEOPLE ARE GROWING MORE EDUCATED ABOUT THE IMPORTANCE OF PROTECTING THESE BEAUTIFUL ANIMALS!

YOU CAN JOIN THESE GROUPS ON THIS VERY SPECIAL MISSION BY VISITING THEM ON THE INTERNET --

HTTP://WWW.SAVETIGERSNOW.ORG/
HTTP://WWW.PLANETE-TIGRE.ORG/